Short Circuit

by Olga Litowinsky

interior illustrations by
Don Morrison

STECK-VAUGHN
ELEMENTARY · SECONDARY · ADULT · LIBRARY

A Harcourt Company

www.steck-vaughn.com

ISBN 0-8114-9323-7

    6 7 8 9 01 00

Produced by Mega-Books of New York, Inc.
Design and Art Direction by Michaelis/Carpelis Design Assoc.

Cover illustration: Wayne Alfano

CHAPTER
1

"Earthling, prepare to meet your doom!"

Andy Clayton laughed. "That's what you think, Fred. I'm in top form. I've been getting ready for our camping trip for days!"

"We'll see how fit you are tomorrow," answered Andy's friend, Fred Emerson. He paused for a moment. "Sorry, Andy, a customer just came into the store. I'll have to call you back."

Fred disappeared from the wallcom screen. The wallcom was a combination of a computer, a telephone, a TV, and a remote control device. It could be activated by voice or by hand. Every room in the house had one.

Andy pressed a button. The wallcom's dial tone went off and music came on. Andy pressed another switch on the wallcom, and his list of camping equipment popped up on the split screen. He scrolled the list, then said to himself, "Maybe another pair of socks." He went over to the corner.

"Dresser: socks!" Andy cried. Nearly all the furniture in his room was voice-

activated through the wallcom.

A dresser drawer shot open. Andy grabbed a pair of red socks and said, "Dresser: shut up!" He loved doing that. The drawer disappeared into the dresser. Andy stuffed the socks into his backpack.

The wallcom buzzed. Andy turned down the music and pressed the button for the phone.

Fred's smiling face came up on the screen. He was an old friend of Andy's father, who had died when Andy was a baby. Fred had been like a second father to Andy for as long as Andy could remember.

"Hi, Andy," Fred said. "Sorry about the interruption."

"No problem," said Andy. "What time should I be at the store tomorrow?" the boy asked.

"Just after sunrise," Fred replied. "I want to get out before any customers show up. Now that it's almost summer the tourists are—"

The screen went blank.

"That's weird," Andy thought. He pressed several buttons but the screen remained blank. "I wonder if it's a power failure?" he said aloud.

Andy snatched his battery-powered pokcom pocket computer from his desk and flicked the 'on' switch. Nothing. He threw the pokcom on the bed and raced downstairs.

"Mom, can I use your pokcom?" he asked. His mother was standing at the kitchen counter, staring at the robochef and yelling, "Add the carrots!" She turned to Andy. "This is strange," she said. "The robochef was mixing the ingredients for carrot cake, but when it came time to add the freeze-dried carrots, it went off."

"Both my coms are off, too," said Andy. He turned to the refrigerator.

"Fridge: open!" Nothing happened. He pulled on the manual override handle and the door opened. "The light's not on," Andy said.

Ms. Clayton grabbed a package of carrots from the vegetable bin. Then she walked around the kitchen, shouting commands and pressing panels and switches on various appliances. "Nothing's working," she said. "Everything's dead."

"I'll check the circuit breaker," said Andy. He ran down to the basement and opened the panel. He stared at the switches. Each one had been tripped. Andy flipped them back on and looked around to see if the power had come on.

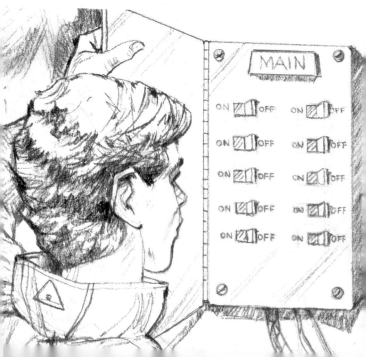

The laundry center was quiet. The Tide-E-Fold clothes sorter was stopped in the middle of folding a T-shirt. There was still no power.

Andy dashed back upstairs. He found his mother standing on the front porch. "Look at those cars," she said. "Nothing's moving." Three cars had stopped on the street. Andy could see the drivers inside.

One of them was waving at him.

It was Ms. Fisher from down the road. She had her dog, a black Belgian shepherd, with her.

Andy dashed over to the car.

"Would you please call the service station?" Ms. Fisher asked. The dog began to bark. "Neither my dashcom nor my pokcom is working, and I can't open the door. All the circuits are dead." Andy could barely hear her through the car window.

"There's been a power failure!"

Andy shouted to the trapped woman.

Ms. Fisher's dog jumped up against the window and barked at Andy.

"How could a power failure affect a battery-operated car?" Ms. Fisher asked Andy, with a frustrated look on her face.

Andy shrugged. That was a good question, a really good question. "I'll see what I can do!" he yelled. Then he headed back to his house.

CHAPTER 2

Andy's front door was locked. Without thinking, Andy pressed his thumb to the electronic plate above the handle and pushed. The door stayed shut. "It can't read my thumbprint with the electricity off," he thought. Andy banged on the door and his mother let him in.

"Thank goodness for manual override," Ms. Clayton said. She sat down in her Ultracomfort armchair, which should have automatically curled itself around her. The chair didn't move. "I wish I knew what was going on," Andy's mother sighed.

Just then there was a banging outside.

"What's that?" Andy asked.

"Someone's at the door," said Ms. Clayton. "I'll get it." She got up and pulled open the front door. It was Vivian Torres, who lived across the street. She and Andy had both grown up on Greenwood Drive and were good friends. Viv smiled at Ms. Clayton.

"I'm locked out," Viv said. "I went outside to help the people in their cars, and now I can't get back into my house. Is it all right if I stay with you for a while? Mom and Dad are working at the hospital and won't be off duty until nine or ten."

"Certainly," answered Ms. Clayton. Viv walked in, just as a buzzer went off in the kitchen. "The robochef!" Ms. Clayton cried. "It's working!" She hurried out of the living room and into the kitchen.

Viv went to the window. "Look! The cars are moving!"

"Wallcom: TV!" Andy said. The screen brightened as the TV came on. A newscaster was speaking.

"For nearly half an hour, the entire Parson Springs area suffered a mysterious shutdown of all normal and emergency electric power. The mayor has asked everyone to remain calm and stay indoors while medical personnel, firefighters, and other authorities deal with emergencies."

The newscaster then began to read from a paper in his hand.

"Fortunately, because of a strike by rocketline pilots, no commercial rockets were in the air. Private flights were grounded while the electronic controls were down. One small rocket en route to Philadelphia was forced to ditch in the Delaware River, and the pilot swam to safety."

"That's probably the first time anyone called a strike fortunate," Andy said.

The newscaster continued. "At Bradley Hospital, the emergency generators failed to work when the main generator went off. Two surgical operations had to be finished by candlelight."

"My parents!" Viv cried. "They must be going crazy taking care of everyone!"

A TV crew member hurried up to the newscaster and handed him another piece of paper. He quickly scanned the page then read it aloud.

"This just in: A short circuit at the zoo caused the electronically controlled cages to open. Many animals are on the loose, roaming through the Parson Springs area. Flocks of exotic birds have been spotted across the city. A

chimpanzee was found playing with a child in a nearby backyard."

"Wow. I know this is serious, but it's kind of funny, too," said Viv. "Why don't you go after the birds with your birdcalls, Andy?"

"I don't know exotic birdcalls, only native birdcalls," Andy said. He frowned. "Do you suppose the zoo will ever get those birds back?"

"Maybe some of them will return to their nests at the zoo," said Ms. Clayton, coming back into the living room.

By now the TV newscaster was repeating the earlier warning about staying indoors. "TV: Shut up!" Andy commanded. The picture disappeared.

"Why do you act so bossy with the computers?" Viv asked. "They're only machines."

"Fred taught me that when I was a kid," Andy replied. "He says we have to let them know we're in charge."

"But we are in charge," said Viv. "Besides these computers were made by humans," she added.

Andy shook his head. "Fred says we've let the computers do too much for us. We're forgetting that we're human beings with unique abilities. Hardly anyone knows how to add and subtract, or even cook."

"But why should we bother with those things if computers and robots can do them for us?" Viv asked.

"I don't know exactly," said Andy. "But

I do know I like to work with my hands, build things. And I like to use my head. It feels good."

"I use my head when I do my homework on my computer, and when I give the wallcom and the robots instructions. It's not simple to run all these machines," said Viv.

Andy's mother came in from the kitchen. "Well, I'm glad I know how to do some things by hand," said Ms.

Clayton. "I was in the middle of making a couple of carrot cakes when the robochef shut down. So I just grated some fresh carrots on the old grater Fred gave me." She held up her hands which were covered with carrot peels. "See? They're orange."

"Gross," said Viv. "I hate touching raw food. I'm glad robots deliver it right to the house so the robochef can cook it."

"Speaking of food, why don't you stay for dinner tonight?" Ms. Clayton asked Viv. "We have plenty of tofu lasagna. Or the robochef could make you something else if you like."

"I love lasagna," Viv replied, "and carrot cake! Thanks for inviting me. I don't want to go home alone. I still feel a little creepy about that power failure."

"So do I," said Andy. "I'm glad I'm going camping tomorrow with Fred." He laughed. "There's not much chance of a power failure in the woods!"

CHAPTER 3

After dinner, Viv, Andy and his mother went into the living room. Ms. Clayton sat in her chair and leaned back as its arms cradled her. "I'm glad the chair is working again," she said.

"I wonder if they've found out what caused the blackout," Andy said. "Maybe it was a freak lightning storm somewhere."

Viv sat down on the sofa. "I'll bet it was aliens," she said.

"Aliens? Yeah, right," Andy said sarcastically. "And I'm one myself. My other head's upstairs."

Viv picked up a cushion and aimed it

at Andy. "Do you want to take a fast trip to the moon?" asked Viv.

"Maybe," Andy said, guarding himself against the cushion Viv held over her head. "But in a spaceship, not as a human asteroid."

"What's the matter with you two?" Ms. Clayton asked. "All you do is argue." Viv dropped the cushion and Andy sat down beside her.

"That's better." Ms. Clayton settled back and looked at her watch. "Wallcom: *Sara Peel Reports*!" she said.

The TV program came on. Sara Peel was in the middle of her introduction to the night's show. "Joining us will be a panel of scientists who will discuss the

mysterious power failures that have been plaguing the eastern part of the country for the past two days. All electronic circuits and microchips were affected. Everything from atomic power stations to toys."

"Microchips?" Ms. Clayton asked. "That's impossible." Andy and Viv leaned forward, eager to hear what the panel members had to say.

"Our first guest is Nich Price," Sara

Peel continued, "an electrical engineer at ConPower in New Jersey."

Nich Price, a slender gray-haired man, began to speak. "In many respects these breakdowns are similar to the massive electric failures in Honolulu in 1962. Those failures were caused by an atomic test that took place 800 miles away from the islands, over the Pacific."

Sara Peel broke in. "Do you mean to say these breakdowns are the result of a nuclear explosion?" she asked.

"We don't know," answered Mr. Price. "That's what makes this so bizarre."

"How can a nuclear blast affect microchips?" Sara Peel asked.

"A nuclear blast can cause an electromagnetic pulse, or EMP, that travels at the speed of light," Mr. Price explained. "This pulse knocks the electricity out from its sources, and drains those sources of any power."

"How does that affect human lives?"

Sara Peel asked her guest.

"Well, the pulse itself passes through people," Mr. Price replied. "It wouldn't affect us unless we were touching metal or an electrical appliance. The electrons go right to anything metal, such as microchips, and cause a kind of giant short circuit."

"So are you saying that's what happened?" Sara Peel asked.

"That's my theory," replied Mr. Price. "But the catch is, we've had no reports of a nuclear explosion since the Peruvian tests back in the year 2034."

"Thank you, Mr. Price." Sara Peel turned to the camera. "Our second guest is Tomoe Abe, professor of physics at the University of Tokyo."

A middle-aged woman smiled into the camera. "I'm sorry to say that, like Mr. Price, I have no idea what caused these failures. However, electrons can be stripped from atoms in machines like the particle accelerator in Chiba, Japan."

"Does stripping the electrons cause power failures?" asked Sara Peel.

Dr. Abe shook her head. "It shouldn't," she replied. "The particle accelerators are shielded. Also, I have no idea how anyone could generate a pulse as strong as Mr. Price described."

"Quite so, Dr. Abe," said Sara Peel. "Thank you."

She turned to the camera. "Our final guest is Felicity Rasmussen, professor of astronomy at the University of California." Sara Peel faced Professor Rasmussen. "As I understand it, Professor, you and your colleagues have made some, shall we say, extraordinary observations."

Professor Rasmussen started to give Sara Peel a reply. "During the past few days," she began, "astronomers around the world have been sighting unusual green flashes in the sky. We think they are signals from the Andromeda galaxy. It is our theory that these are most certainly signs of intelligent life in space."

"But we've been searching for years and not once found any proof of alien life," said Sara Peel.

"We haven't been looking in the right places," explained the professor. "And no one's been willing to believe the

evidence we do have, that aliens arrived
here over a hundred years ago. They're
right under our noses." Professor
Rasmussen leaned forward and stared
into the camera. "Earth people!" she
shouted, "We have been invaded by—"

The screen went blank. "Not another
power failure!" Andy cried.

A notice came up on the screen.
"Please stand by," it read.

Andy chuckled. "I'll bet they're
dragging that professor out the door of

the TV studio right now," he said.

"It's not funny, Andy," said Viv. "They don't want us to hear what the professor has to say."

"Come on, Viv!" Andy protested. "That woman has seen too many science fiction videos. Space aliens! When they don't know how to explain something, they always blame aliens."

"But suppose it's aliens who are causing the power failures?" Viv persisted.

"Wallcom: off!" said Ms. Clayton, interrupting their argument. Through the window she saw a car pull up across the street. "Your parents are home, Viv."

"I'd better get going." Viv got up from the sofa and went to the door.

"I'll walk you home," Andy offered, standing up.

"I can make it by myself. I don't see any aliens on the street," Viv answered curtly. Then she turned to Andy's

mother. "Good night, Ms. Clayton.
Thanks for a great dinner."

Viv walked down the steps of the
Claytons' front porch. Then she stopped
and turned toward Andy, standing at the

front door. "Enjoy your camping trip, Andy," said Viv. "I'll see you when you get back. We have a discussion to finish."

Andy watched Viv cross the street and walk into her house. Then he stared up at the sky. Where was the Andromeda galaxy anyway? Could there really be aliens out there?

CHAPTER 4

The next morning Andy parked his electric bike behind Fred's store and walked in. "Good morning, Fred," he called out to his friend.

Fred was sitting at his desk in the back room. "Good to see you, Andy. I'm almost ready," he replied.

Fred ran an old general store that had once been in the center of a small village. Farm families had bought all their goods there back in the 1800s. But by the beginning of the year 2000, the farms were long gone. Most of the old houses and stores in the village had been torn down and replaced with apartment complexes. The city council had made the store an official landmark, a kind of "museum of the past."

Fred sold a few groceries and always had a pot of fresh coffee on the converted electric "woodstove," but he made his living from selling antiques.

Andy checked the shelves while he waited for Fred. Lying between an old electric drill and a kerosene lamp was a clunky old TV set from the 1990s. Andy

picked up the remote, looked at the price tag, and quickly put it back down.

"All right, let's get the show on the road," Fred said. "I want to be out of here before customers start knocking on the door and wondering why I'm closed."

Fred and Andy got into Fred's modified classic Dodge Ram pickup. Fred pushed some buttons on the dashcom, then drove down the side streets until he got to the Magway ramp. Then he sat back as the truck clicked into place above the magnetic rail and let the robopilot do the work.

Fred turned to Andy. "Were you and your mother okay during the power failure yesterday?" he asked. "I would have called you back, but things got chaotic at the store."

"We weren't affected too much," replied Andy. Mom was in the middle of making a couple of carrot cakes. "When the robochef went down, Mom had to use fresh carrots and the grater you gave her. She seemed to get a kick out of it. Luckily the power came back on in time for the robochef to bake the cakes. One carrot cake is for you, Fred. It's tucked away in my backpack."

Fred grinned. "How about a piece for breakfast?"

"I was hoping you'd ask." Andy dug into his backpack and pulled out the carrot cake.

"Dee-licious," Fred said after

swallowing the last of his slice. "Those robots can't make a cake like this. Mind you, theirs is pretty good, but nothing beats homemade and humanmade."

Fred nodded at Andy. "It's what I keep telling you. Don't forget your basic skills. Machines can't do everything."

"Is that why we're going camping?"

"We must never forget where we came from," Fred said in a serious tone. "Our ancestors worked hard, but they thought of nature as their enemy, so they did their best to conquer it. In the process they destroyed most of it. Now we have to travel huge distances just to see a real forest. And even the forests we have aren't what they used to be."

Fred paused a moment as they sped past a stretch of old factories beside the Magway. Then he continued. "We can't drink the polluted water in the streams or eat any fish that might still be in them. We can't even build a fire with

wood from the trees because wood is so scarce. And besides, with all the pollution, wood fires aren't allowed anymore."

"So why are we going?" Andy asked.

"Because we can still sleep under the stars and feel the wind on our skin," answered Fred. "Which reminds me, did you put on your sunblock? The ultraviolet level is high these days."

"I wear it all the time," replied Andy.

And I'll put on my sunglasses when we get out of the truck."

"So will I," said Fred. "The polarized windshield of my Dodge Ram is enough protection for right now."

They rode along in silence until the dashcom beeper signaled they were approaching the exit ramp. Fred took hold of the wheel when the Magway switched them off the main Magrail. He shifted the truck back into manual as he steered it down the ramp.

It wasn't long before the two campers were at the entrance to the park. Fred drove into the underground parking garage. The garage could hold a thousand cars, but today it was empty. Most people preferred to spend their spare time at the malls or the Fantasy Worlds.

Andy himself occasionally went to the Fantasy Worlds with Viv. The huge, domed amusement parks re-created famous places where people could surf in "Hawaii" or even climb "Mount Everest." But Andy was glad he would be hiking on a real mountain for a change.

He heaved his backpack onto his shoulders. Fred slid a plastic card into a slot by their parking space. The slot activated an electronic field to protect his truck. His bank account was automatically charged with the parking fee.

Andy and Fred took the elevator to

the ground level and came up in the park store.

Using his plastic card again, Fred bought two frozen soybean tofu trout from the electronic display and an artificial campfire kit. The campfire kit used a chemical fuel that burned like a real fire. But unlike wood fires, the chemicals turned carbon dioxide into oxygen, so the fire didn't pollute the air. Scientists had gotten this idea from observing green plants.

"The trout will defrost by the time we reach a good place for setting up camp," Fred told Andy. "Let's go."

CHAPTER 5

"Wow, I don't think we've seen a single person the whole time we've been out here," Andy observed. It was after noon, and he and Fred were well on their way up Eagle Mountain .

"That's fine with me," said Fred. "I see too many people back at the store. These days, it seems like all people want to do is shop."

They continued to hike along the trail, listening to the birds and trying to identify them. Fred pointed quickly to a tree. "Look," he said. A screech drowned out the tuneful birdsong they had been listening to.

"What's that?" Andy asked Fred, who was squinting his eyes, trying to look up the trail.

"It's behind those trees up ahead," Fred said, pointing again.

Andy heard the screech once more.

"Now it sounds as if it's coming from those bushes." Andy stared into the woods. Then he began to laugh. "It's you screeching! You got me again, Fred. Where did you get that screech?"

Fred broke into a big smile. "From an Amazon parrot. I thought you might believe it was one of those birds that escaped from the zoo."

Andy grinned. "It sounded more like a bobcat up a tree. How did you throw your voice?" Andy asked. "I've been practicing my ventriloquism, but I sure can't throw my voice that well. Maybe you can give me some pointers."

Fred shifted his backpack. "Let's stop for lunch. I'll give you a lesson . . . and we can have some more of that carrot cake for dessert!"

They found a clearing on the other side of some bushes and spread out the food.

"We should get back to work," said a muffled voice. The voice came from the trail below the clearing. Andy looked at Fred, who was taking a bite of his sandwich. "Hey Fred, didn't anyone ever tell you not to talk with your mouth full?" he asked.

"That wasn't me," Fred said. "I'm not that good at throwing my voice."

Andy turned and heard an electric motor humming on the trail. Through a gap in the bushes he saw two people in a four-wheel drive speeding past them.

"What's that car doing up here?" asked Andy. "That's illegal!"

"Could be a ranger vehicle," Fred suggested. He began to pack. "Let's finish eating on the trail and save the

carrot cake for dinner. Come on, we still
have a way to go to get to the top."

Andy was glad to move on. He began
to walk fast.

"Slow down," Fred said after a while.
"You'll tire me out. After all, we are
hiking up a mountain!"

"Sorry," Andy said, slowing down. "So
what do you think caused the power
failure? Did you watch *Sara Peel Reports*
last night?"

Fred nodded. "It was interesting, but I wish they hadn't cut off that astronomer."

"Don't tell me you believe in aliens, too!" exclaimed Andy.

Fred looked at Andy. "Too?" he asked.

"Viv. She thinks aliens might have caused the breakdown. We had a fight over it."

"Look at it this way, Andy," Fred said. "It's statistically possible. With millions

of galaxies in the universe, there could be other solar systems that have planets with conditions favorable to life."

"Okay, I accept that," Andy agreed. But would that life have evolved enough to travel through space?"

"Don't forget the latest theory is that the universe was created in one big bang ten to twenty billion years ago," Fred answered. "Life could have gotten a headstart on another planet. The beings there could be more advanced than we are. It's possible they might have perfected intergalactic travel by now."

"But if they came here, why don't we know about it?" Andy asked.

"People have been reporting aliens for years," Fred said. "But the government and the media have always made people who talked about aliens look foolish. My great-grandmother said she saw a flying saucer once."

Andy snickered. "Filled with little green men?" he asked.

"See what I mean?" Fred replied. "My great-grandmother was a no-nonsense, intelligent person. Her husband, my great-grandfather, worked for a law firm on Wall Street. He saw the saucer, too. It hovered over their street for a few minutes, then it swooped off."

"And you believe that story?"

"Let's just say I don't disbelieve it,"

Fred answered slowly.

"So did your great-grandparents report what they saw?" Andy asked.

"My great-grandfather would have lost his job if he went around Wall Street talking about flying saucers."

"Hmm, that would have been around 1960, right?" Andy asked. "If the aliens came here that long ago, where are they now?"

"Remind me to show you an old newspaper clipping from the twentieth century when we get back home," Fred said. "It reported that aliens had been captured and were being hidden in Oklahoma by the military."

"But why?" Andy wanted to know. People have a right to know if aliens are here on Earth, don't they?"

"The government's afraid of a panic," explained Fred. "Ever hear of the Orson Welles radio broadcast in 1938, about an invasion from Mars?"

Andy shook his head. Fred went on. "Welles was a famous director and actor. He based a radio show on H. G. Wells's story, *The War of the Worlds*, and made it seem as if Martians landed in Grover's Mills, a town in New Jersey."

"Like a hoax?" Andy asked.

"Not really," Fred replied. "Welles never expected people to take the radio program seriously. But they did and people all over the country panicked. Do you think if we heard aliens had landed it would be any different today?"

"I don't know," Andy said, shrugging his shoulders. "The idea is creepy—not because the aliens would be different from us, we could get used to that. But if they were able to get to Earth, it would mean they were more powerful than we. We wouldn't know how to handle it."

"Precisely," said Fred.

CHAPTER
6

"But hey, we came out here to enjoy ourselves, not talk about aliens," Fred said, pointing up toward the trees. "Look, a cardinal!"

Andy whipped out his binoculars. A red bird was flying past a stand of oaks. Andy whistled. The call was perfect and the sound carried through the mountain air. The cardinal alighted on a branch, looked around, and returned the call. Andy smiled.

"You must have been practicing," said Fred.

"It's fun!" Andy said. "Listen. Can you guess this one?" Andy whistled again.

"Baltimore oriole. Let's hear more."

They took turns trying out different birdcalls as they continued up the trail. Then Fred watched as Andy practiced talking without moving his lips.

"You're getting good," Fred said.

"But how do you throw your voice?" Andy asked.

"Ventriloquists don't really throw their voices," Fred said. "They know how to adjust their voices so they sound distant, but they really make you think the voice is far away by using misdirection."

"What do you mean?" asked Andy .

"When you heard the screech earlier, I was already pointing ahead, and so you expected the sound to come from there. That's misdirection," Fred explained.

"I'd like to practice that," Andy said.

"Go ahead," urged Fred.

Time passed quickly while Andy practiced. At last they reached the campsite. Andy threw down his backpack and stretched.

Fred tossed the fire kit and packaged tofu trout onto the ground and slid off his backpack. He walked over to the stream. "I sure wish we could have fresh trout, and a wood fire to cook them on." He sat down on a rock, took off his shoes, and rubbed his feet. "My dogs are barking. I'm going to soak them for a while."

"This is great country," said Andy. "Can we wait to set up camp? I'd like to climb to the top of Eagle Mountain to see the sunset."

"Go ahead. I'll have everything shipshape when you get back," Fred said. "I just need to let my feet rest for a second in this nice cold water. It feels great."

Andy headed up the path beside the stream. It was shady among the pines and birch trees, so he took off the sunglasses he'd been wearing. Using his

binoculars, Andy spotted a few more birds and practiced throwing calls. The air smelled so clean and fresh, Andy felt energized and walked faster.

The hiking trail ended at a ledge below the summit. Andy stopped, sat down on the ledge and gazed westward at the view.

He could see Parson Springs in the distance. The domes of the Fantasy Worlds were glowing pink in the setting sun. The cars traveling on the Magways had their lights on already and looked

like glowing red and white beads moving on invisible strings.

The sun sank below the horizon and Andy realized he'd better get back to the camp.

As he turned, Andy glanced up at the mountain's summit and saw a tower reflecting the sun's orange afterglow. A boulder had blocked the tower from Andy's view as he'd come up the trail earlier.

"That's weird," he said to himself. "I wonder what that is? And what's it doing up there?" Andy switched on his belt laserlight and began to climb to the summit. He wanted to get a closer look at the tower.

Andy scrambled to get to the very top of the mountain, which was almost bare rock. Boulders were scattered about, but there were no trees. The tower had four legs and stood on a patch of scruffy grass.

The tower was only a few feet taller than Andy. It looked like a miniature of the Eiffel Tower. He touched it, expecting the coldness of metal. But the tower's shiny sand-colored material felt more like plastic. That was the last thing Andy felt before something crashed down on his head.

CHAPTER 7

"He's only a kid, Talon," Andy heard as he came to. Waves of pain rolled through his head. He lay still on the ground, eyes closed, trying to remember what had happened. Slowly Andy's memory returned. He'd been examining the tower when he felt a blow on his head. Someone had knocked him out and left him lying on the ground.

"Should I open my eyes? No, better to wait and play dead," Andy told himself, "until I find out what's going on." The pain in his head made him want to let out a groan, but he suppressed it.

"He may be just a kid, Bray, but kids

talk," said another voice, a woman's.
"We can't let him go. But what we can
do is shove him off the mountain.
Everybody will just think he fell."

"We're not supposed to kill
Earthlings, Talon," Bray said.

"Let's not argue," replied Talon. "It's
time to turn on the electron stripper."

Andy felt someone brush against his

leg. Then he heard a loud hum.

"It's working like a charm!" said the man called Bray. "Parson Springs is powerless!"

The woman laughed. "In more ways than one," she said. Andy heard static. "The New York group is reporting," Talon said to her companion. "Listen."

Still trying to play as if he were unconscious, Andy strained to hear the voice through the static and the hum from the tower.

"Talon and Bray, here in New York at the Empire State Building, we are still having problems with the tower aimed at Brooklyn and Long Island. New York is a big city with too many tall buildings. We may have to set up another tower at the World Trade Center."

"I told them so," Bray commented.

"But our regional experiment is still a success," said yet another voice. "Most of the electron strippers in the northeast are in place and operational. We can take Washington without a struggle whenever we're ready." The voices stopped.

"We've got a long way to go before we have electron strippers in every major Earth city," Talon said. "But it will happen in less than a year, now that we're sure it can be done. Then our brothers and sisters on Panykros will arrive in full force!"

"I wish my grandparents were still alive. They dreamed of the day Earth would be made our colony," said Bray.

"Your grandparents and mine were heroes and pioneers," Talon replied. "They came here and hoped to find safety from the increasing cold on Panykros. But the Earth people rejected them, mocked them, and locked them up so no one could hear their story. We had to travel to Earth secretly."

"Yes," Bray agreed. He laughed meanly. "And since the Earthlings would not welcome us to their planet, we have no choice. We'll invade."

Aliens! Andy was stunned. And he was their prisoner! Andy was tempted to open his eyes so that he could see what they looked like.

"We must," Talon nodded gravely, "to save all Panykrosians." The alien's voice sounded to Andy as if she'd moved to the edge of the summit. "It is no more than ten degrees at the Panykros equator now," said Talon. "Our people need a warm home like Earth."

"But in the last hundred years they've nearly destroyed the Earth our grandparents knew. Just about every inch has been overdeveloped. Even the seas are covered with floating cities," said Bray.

Talon shrugged. "What other choice do we have? It was a good thing the

Earth people became so dependent on electronics," she continued. "It made it easy for us," said Talon.

"They'll hate being the subjects of aliens," Bray said. "How strange that the Earthlings' technological advances led to their doom."

"It's even stranger," Talon added, "that our electron stripper taps into Earth's magnetic field. We're using Earth people's own magnetic force lines to attack their equipment!"

"They can't help it if they're so backward," Bray replied. "After all, we evolved first. They still have five toes!"

Andy judged by the aliens' voices that they weren't near him now. He cautiously opened his eyes. The moon had come up, and Andy could see the two aliens were looking over the countryside. They were not paying attention to him.

Both of them had long, pale faces and nearly white hair. They looked somewhat human, Andy thought, but their proportions were odd. They seemed to be well built on top, but their legs were very short.

"What about the boy?" asked Bray. "Don't forget, Talon. We come from an advanced race. We do not kill without good reason."

Talon turned to look at Andy, who quickly closed his eyes again. "We'll have to ask for instructions at dawn when the experiment is over," the alien said. "Let's tie him up now and wait. He's still unconscious, but he may wake up at any moment." Bray nodded.

The aliens dragged Andy down the rocky path. He pretended to be unconscious while they propped his limp body against a tree.

"After this, we can catch some sleep in the car," Bray said to Talon.

Andy felt a soft wire being wrapped around his body. "Oh great," he thought, "I'll never get away now."

CHAPTER
8

Andy leaned his head against the tree. He couldn't move. He looked at the wire and wondered if it was made from the same plastic-like material as the tower.

He heard a birdcall in the woods. It was a cardinal. That was strange. Cardinals slept at night. He heard the call again.

Andy answered it. The cardinal called once more, and Andy answered it again. He heard a rustling in the bushes and then Fred grabbed his shoulders.

"Am I glad to see you!" Andy cried.

Fred cut the wire and helped Andy to stand up. Andy 's legs felt shaky.

"We've got to stay off the trail," Fred
warned. "I don't think the aliens heard
me, but let's wait a minute to be sure.
Their car is parked down the hill, deep
in the bushes."

Fred held up his hand. Andy heard
the wind rustling through the pines, the
chatter of the stream and Fred's heavy
breathing.

"It's okay," Fred said finally. "I got

worried when you didn't come back to camp, so I headed up the trail to find you. Then I saw two people going into some bushes and followed them to a car."

"That's probably the car I saw on the trail," said Andy.

"You were right to worry then," Fred replied. "Those two definitely weren't rangers. I thought about going up to them to ask if they'd seen you, but then I heard them say something about their prisoner! So, as soon as they got in their car, I went back up the trail and discovered the tower, but no sign of you. That's when I decided to try the cardinal call. What's going on?"

"They're aliens, Fred! They want to take over the Earth! We've got to get help!" cried Andy. He quickly filled Fred in about what he'd heard.

"Do you have your pokcom?" asked Fred. "Mine's not working. . . I wanted a couple of days off from that thing. But it looks like we could use it right now."

Andy pulled out his pokcom. "Here it is," said Andy, as he switched it on and off. "But it isn't working, see? It's because of that tower! It's stealing all of our power! And who knows what else it can do!"

Fred scratched his head thoughtfully. "What do you say we go back to the tower?" he asked.

Andy felt the bump on his head from where he'd been hit. The last thing he wanted to do was go back there.

Suddenly Andy heard a plane overhead. Just as suddenly a ray beam shot out from the mountain top. The plane disappeared.

Fred and Andy looked at each other. "Let's go," Andy said grimly. The two of them started up the trail.

When they reached the summit, they heard the tower still humming. Fred ducked behind the boulder, and Andy followed. Fred held his finger to his lips.

"I've got something to tell you, Andy,"

he whispered. "Professor Rasmussen was telling the truth. The government knows we're being invaded, but they're trying to keep it quiet."

Andy stared at Fred. "They know?"

"Remember when I told you about the newspaper clippings? It's true. Aliens first came here over a hundred and fifty years ago," Fred continued. "They looked human enough to blend in with our population. I know this because I'm a member of a secret government agency that has been tracking reports of aliens for decades."

Andy studied Fred's eyes. He had known this man all his life. His father had known him, too. How could Fred have hidden such a big part of himself from Andy all this time?

Andy looked down at the pitch black expanse of land that was his hometown. Was there really a chance to save everyone from these aliens?

"That tower's got to go," Fred said, his eyes full of worry.

"You're right. We've got to stop them!" Andy cried in agreement.

Fred slapped Andy on the shoulder. "That's my boy. Once the tower is turned off and my pokcom's running, I'll get in touch with the agency. They'll send rocketcopters out here within minutes to capture these aliens. And they'll head

out in full force to stop the others. I'll also call the Parson Springs Gazette and get a reporter out here. It's time we took some action and let people know what we're up against."

Fred studied the tower for a moment, looking for a control panel. But there was nothing to be found. "You'd be surprised how many people in Parson Springs are involved with the underground agency, including your friend, Viv," Fred said.

"Viv?" Andy looked stunned. "So that's why she got so mad when I told her I thought she was off the wall about aliens!"

"Naturally," Fred replied. "I'm used to it, but she's still young and finds it hard to be misunderstood."

Andy looked thoughtful for a moment. "I have a plan." He whispered eagerly into Fred 's ear.

Fred nodded. "Let's get to work."

Andy and Fred gathered as many rocks as they could carry.

Fred stayed behind the boulder as Andy tiptoed past the tower to a boulder on the other side of it. Andy hooted like an owl. Fred hooted back. They were ready.

"Hey, Andy," Fred shouted, throwing both the rocks and his voice toward the tower. From a distance, the rocks sounded like footsteps at the base of the tower. "Where are you?" He threw some more rocks.

"Over here," said Andy as he tossed a few rocks toward the base of the tower. Within moments Andy heard someone scrambling up the rocky path.

"Don't move!" cried Talon as the two aliens ran up to the tower.

"There's nobody here," said Bray, stopping in his tracks. He looked around.

"That's strange," said Talon. "I could

have sworn I heard people up here." She
looked down the trail. "It sounded like
that boy, along with someone else."

Bray went up to the tower and
examined it. He took a remote device
from his pocket and pointed it at the
tower. A control panel opened at the leg
of the tower. "Everything looks okay

here," he said, closing it back up. "But where did all these rocks come from?"

Talon knelt down to study the rocks. An owl hooted. Another returned the owl call.

In an instant Andy and Fred rushed out from behind the boulders and tackled Talon and Bray. The four scuffled on the ground. But the humans had caught the aliens off guard. Within moments Andy and Fred had overpowered the aliens and pinned them to the ground. Using their belts, Andy and Fred tied the aliens' arms behind their backs.

"So you think you're going to take over the Earth, huh?" Andy said to the aliens. "Well, this planet isn't just some Fantasy World for you to do with as you please." Andy took the remote device from Bray and opened the control panel. With the flip of a switch, the humming from the tower stopped.

Andy looked down and saw the lights blink back on in Parson Springs. The red and white beads on the Magway lit up and began moving again.

"What now?" he asked Fred.

"I'll call the agency and get some people out here," Fred said. "But first, take a look at this, Andy." He'd pulled the shoes off Talon's and Bray's feet.

"Four toes on each foot. Back before you were born, Viv's parents had helped out at the scene of a car accident. There was an entire family involved. The Torres saw that each of the family members had four toes on each foot. Viv's parents announced what they had seen in a TV interview. It caused quite a controversy at the time."

"I don't get it," Andy said.

"The Torres' suspected these people were aliens. They'd heard this four-toed theory before. Then the government asked them to keep quiet about it. The Torres have worked with us ever since."

Andy heard a hum. He looked up at the tower. "Oh no! It's still working!"

Fred laughed. "It's your pokcom."

Andy switched it on. Viv's face was on the screen. "Guess what! We had another power failure. You missed it."

"That's what you think!" Andy laughed.